NIGHTMARE WORLD

INTRODUCTION BRIAN PULIDO	P2
"KNEE DEEP IN THE DEAD" WEISBROD – OWEN – REDDINGTON	P3
"THE MILK OF HUMAN KINDNESS" WEISBROD – ROSS – MCKINLEY – REDDINGTON	P11
"HAPPINESS IN SLAVERY" WEISBROD – WINTERS	P19
"TRY HONESTY" WEISBROD – MATLOCK – REDDINGTON	P27
"FOR THOSE ABOUT TO ROCK (WE SALUTE YOU)" WEISBROD – O'GRADY – REDDINGTON	P35
"A SMALL VICTORY" WEISBROD – BOULTWOOD – REDDINGTON	P43
"NOT FOR YOU" WEISBROD – PERRY – JONES – REDDINGTON	P51
"THE WAY I AM" WEISBROD – MILLER – WULF – REDDINGTON	P59
"SLEEP NOW IN THE FIRE" WEISBROD – WELBORN – DREIER – MACKINNON – REDDINGTON	P67
"MOVIN' ON" WEISBROD – DILLON	P75
"WELCOME TO MY NIGHTMARE" WEISBROD – ROSS – 3 – REDDINGTON	P83
"THE MINUTE OF DECAY" WEISBROD – MATLOCK – REDDINGTON	P8
"DISASTERPIECE" WEISBROD – ROSS – MACKINNON – REDDINGTON	

FOR FC9 PUBLISHING
TILMAN GOINS – PRESIDENT/PUBLISHER
RYAN STRATTON – PROJECT MANAGER
LUKE ELLISON – ART DIRECTOR
GREGORY PRICE – WEB DESIGNER

FOR NIGHTMARE WORLD
AARON WEISBROD – WRITER/CREATOR
JAMES REDDINGTON – BOOK DESIGN/LOGOS/LETTERS
KRISTEN PERRY – VOLUME ONE TPB BOOK COVER
RAY DILLON & MARK WINTERS – WEB MONKEYS

NIGHTMARE WORLD: "Knee Deep in the Dead" and Other Tales of Terror. ISBN: 0-9767297-0-9 July 2005. FIRST PRINTING. Published by Funnel Cloud 9, Inc., Morristown, TN. Copyright © 2005 Aaron Weisbrod. All rights reserved. All characters, groups, and their likenesses are trademarks of Aaron Weisbrod. The stories, characters and incidents in this comic are entirely fictional, and any similarities to known persons, living or dead, are purely coincidental. FC9 will not read or accept any unsolicited material or story ideas. PRINTED IN KOREA.

HUNGRY FOR THE DARK

Have a taste for the dark side of things? Like your characters driven and obsessive? Yeah, me too. I don't know where the attraction comes from or where it started. I have my suspicions, but it is there, constantly waiting to be fed. Considering this, when *Aaron Weisbrod's* **Nightmare World** came to my attention, I eagerly devoured the stories.

First launched as a series of stories on the net, you now hold onto **Nightmare World's** debut as a graphic novel. Culled from a plethora of stories, Weisbrod has selected eleven "tales of terror" from *www.NightmareWorld.com* and included two exclusive stories and a few one-page strips to boot.

Several underlying themes come to the surface throughout this collection, though the mood and tone of the stories are as varied as the artwork. These are stories about desperate characters. There's Tim Feasel in "Happiness in Slavery" whose rambling righteous indignation costs him his life? but in an unexpected way. There's the assassin from "A Small Victory" (my personal favorite) who laments his son's death at the hands of a drunk driver. Then there's Gary, the insane cop from "Try Honesty" who has a murderous confession he cannot face-up to telling his partner.

The situations are extreme and routine, strangely at the same time. In "Sleep Now in the Fire" Tammy believes her son's father is Satan and that he's imprisoned them in her suburban home. In "Movin' On" the simple act of hitchhiking takes on murderous proportions while in "The Milk of Human Kindness" a lovers' quarrel in a nightclub turns supernatural.

There is a fun, comedic streak to the tales as Weisbrod sometimes sees hilarity in human suffering. "Knee Deep in the Dead" is a campy parody of the *Friday the 13th* slasher-flicks. "For Those About To Rock (We Salute You)" is a funny take on a Faustian deal with the devil and the single page "Welcome to my Nightmare" provides an insight into Weisbrod's psyche that most of us probably never really wanted to know. (You'll understand what I mean when you read it!)

What we have is a dark smorgasbord to appease the appetite. It would be too narrow to compare **Nightmare World** to *The Twilight Zone* and its anthology format because **Nightmare World** has something *The Twilight Zone* never had, and that's graphic storytelling... that amazing combination of the written word and pictures. Considering this, hats-off to the various artists in this collection as well. Their storytelling is often great and inspired, and I suspect Weisbrod is behind this as well, "casting" his artists to suit each story.

Are you hungry for inspired, off-beat tales of horror and extremes in style? Then **Nightmare World** is your twelve (thirteen?) course meal. Come on in and gorge yourself.

Cordially,

Brian Pulido
Creator/Writer of **Lady Death, Evil Ernie** & a ton of other stuff.

BRIAN PULIDO,
AARON WEISBROD,
AND STEVE HUGHES
(TOLEDO, OHIO, 1995)

HAPPINESS IN SLAVERY
WRITTEN BY AARON WEISBROD
FULLY ILLUSTRATED AND LETTERED BY MARK WINTERS

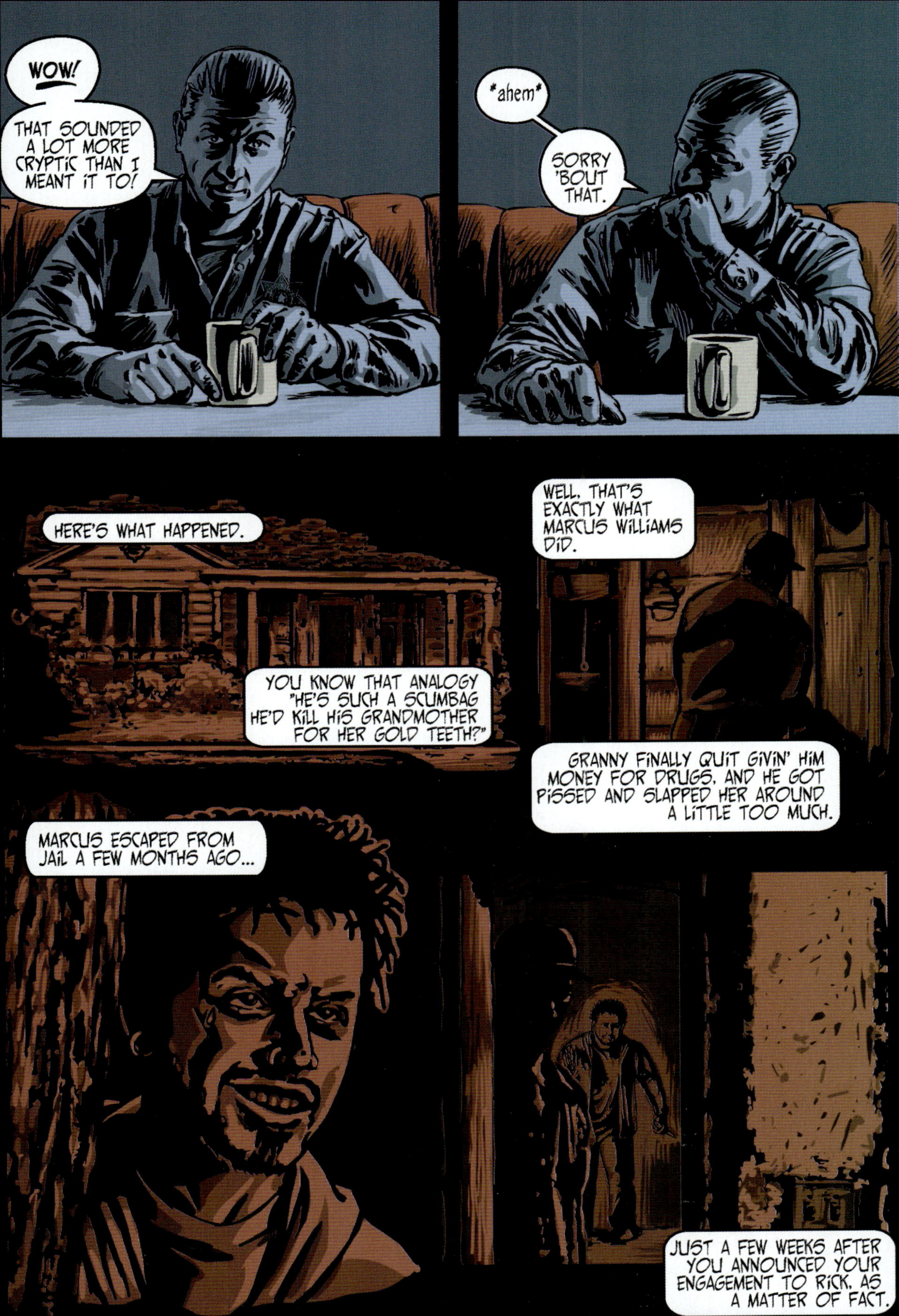

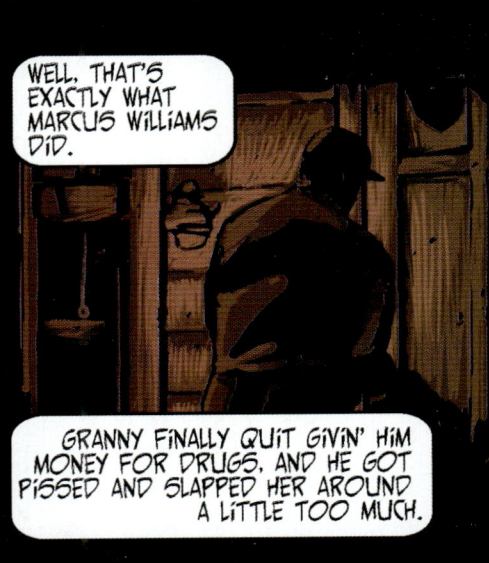

SOMEHOW MARCUS GOT IT IN HIS HEAD THAT RICK WAS AN EASY MARK WITH A LOT OF CASH IN HIS HOUSE...

WELL...

SO HE CASED THE HOUSE UNTIL RICK CAME HOME AND...

YOU KNOW WHAT HAPPENED NEXT.

MARCUS THOUGHT THAT IT WOULD BE AN EASY IN AND OUT JOB. BUT THERE'S ONE THING HE WASN'T EXPECTING...

CRACK!

AND THAT WOULD BE ONE OF NEW ORLEAN'S FINEST ALREADY THERE WAITING FOR HIM.

FINALLY...

I CAN MAKE MY DREAM COME TRUE!

OH, GREAT SATAN, HE WHO IS RESPONSIBLE FOR ALL HEAVY METAL...
SPEED METAL, DEATH METAL, GRIND-CORE, ANGST METAL...
THE OCCASIONAL HEAVY ALTERNATIVE ROCK RADIO SINGLE, AND ALL OTHER MUSIC THAT DOES NOT SUCK...
SEE MY SACRIFICE! HEAR MY PLEA!
GRANT ME AN AUDIENCE WITH YOU SO I MAY OFFER YOU MY SOUL IN EXCHANGE FOR THAT WHICH I DESIRE MOST...
THE CHANCE TO BECOME A HUGE ROCK STAR LIKE DAISY DAHMER!
YES! YES!
YESSSSSSSSSSSSSSSS!!!
SATAN?

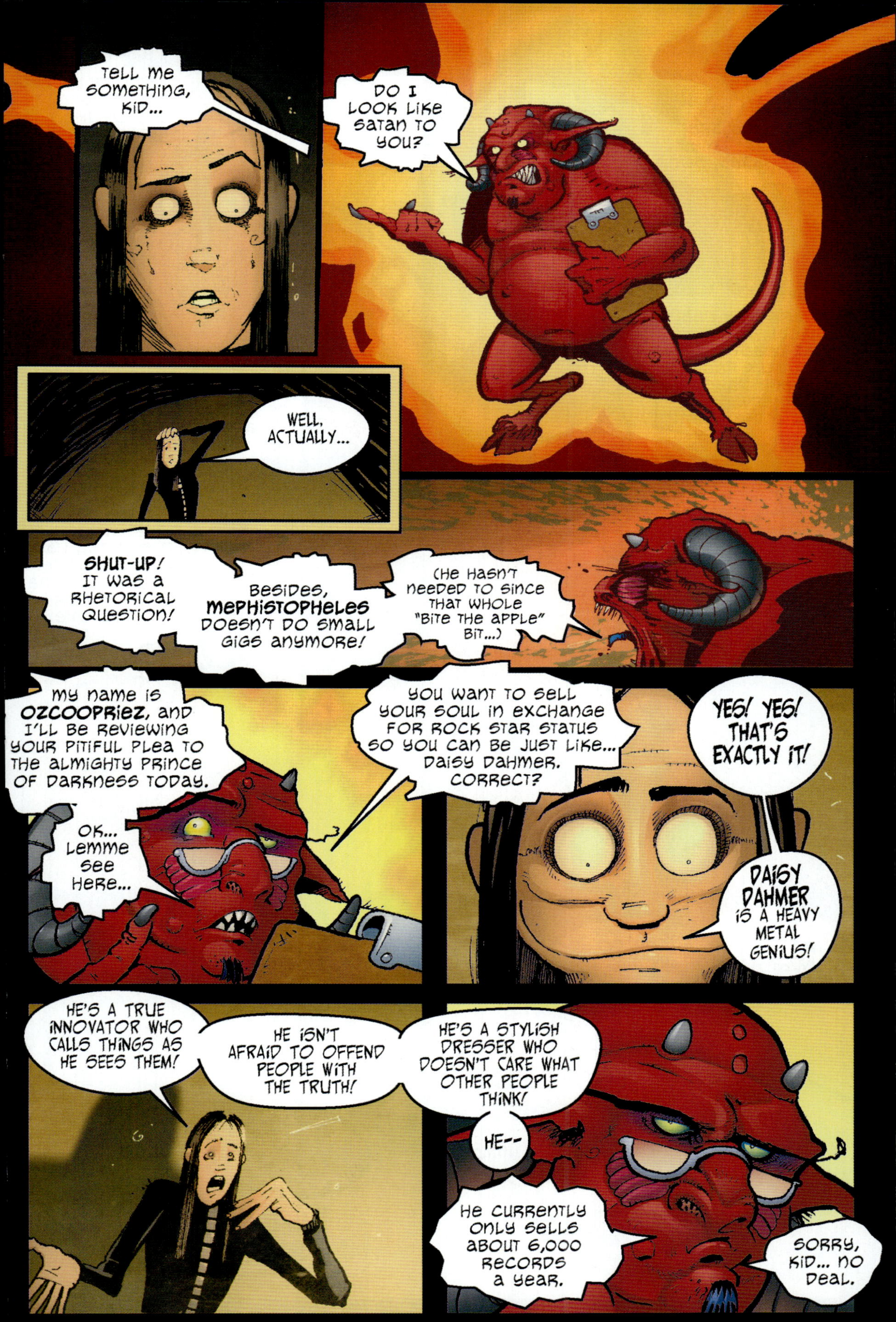
TELL ME SOMETHING, KID...
DO I LOOK LIKE SATAN TO YOU?
WELL, ACTUALLY...
SHUT-UP! IT WAS A RHETORICAL QUESTION!
BESIDES, MEPHISTOPHELES DOESN'T DO SMALL GIGS ANYMORE!
(HE HASN'T NEEDED TO SINCE THAT WHOLE "BITE THE APPLE" BIT...)
MY NAME IS OZCOOPRIEZ, AND I'LL BE REVIEWING YOUR PITIFUL PLEA TO THE ALMIGHTY PRINCE OF DARKNESS TODAY.
OK... LEMME SEE HERE...
YOU WANT TO SELL YOUR SOUL IN EXCHANGE FOR ROCK STAR STATUS SO YOU CAN BE JUST LIKE... DAISY DAHMER. CORRECT?
YES! YES! THAT'S EXACTLY IT!
DAISY DAHMER IS A HEAVY METAL GENIUS!
HE'S A TRUE INNOVATOR WHO CALLS THINGS AS HE SEES THEM!
HE ISN'T AFRAID TO OFFEND PEOPLE WITH THE TRUTH!
HE'S A STYLISH DRESSER WHO DOESN'T CARE WHAT OTHER PEOPLE THINK!
HE--
HE CURRENTLY ONLY SELLS ABOUT 6,000 RECORDS A YEAR.
SORRY, KID... NO DEAL.

WHAT?!?
These are tough times in Hades, son.
The Lord of the Flies can't go around granting the requests of anyone who's offering up their soul, you know?
The Dark One needs musical acts who can at least achieve a platinum record these days. Otherwise, what's the point?
Especially considering all of the internet-based music piracy going on these days!
I'll tell you what... the archfiend has a very special circle of hell reserved for the bastard who started that phenomenon!
BUT... BUT... BUT I KILLED SOMEONE AND EVERYTHING!
Him?
The internet cartoonist?!?
Don?t worry: Old Scratch has had an oversized blender set aside for him for a long time.
NO! YOU DON'T UNDERSTAND!
I'LL DO ANYTHING TO BE A ROCK STAR!
ANYTHING!
Did you just say "anything"?

AND THAT'S HOW I GOT TO WHERE I AM TODAY.

KEITH SHIMBORSKE

I'M NOW A MUSICAL CELEBRITY AND PART OF ONE OF THE BEST SELLING BANDS IN THE WORLD.

I HAVE MY OWN TOUR BUS, MY OWN WARDROBE CONSULTANT, MY OWN PERSONAL ASSISTANT...

HERE'S YOUR BOTTLED WATER, MR. SHIMBORSKE!

YOU'RE SET TO TAKE THE STAGE WITH THE GUYS IN LESS THAN TWO MINUTES!

EVEN MY OWN GROUPIES!

GOOD LUCK, KEITH.

WE'LL BE WAITING FOR YOU AFTER THE SHOW.

I'M LIVING MY DREAM.

WAITING UNTIL THE LAST SECOND AS USUAL, I SEE?

REMEMBER... THE VOICE TRACKS WILL START IN EXACTLY... TWENTY-FOUR SECONDS!

IT'S TRUE THAT THINGS DIDN'T WORK OUT EXACTLY THE WAY I HAD ORIGINALLY ENVISIONED THEY WOULD...

BUT THAT'S OK.

ALL THAT MATTERS IS THAT, AT LONG LAST, I'VE FINALLY DONE IT...

I'M FINALLY A ROCK STAR.

GLAMOR BOYZ

A SMALL VICTORY
WRITTEN BY AARON WEISBROD
FULLY ILLUSTRATED BY DAN BOULTWOOD
LETTERING BY JAMES REDDINGTON
PLEAS
Do not dis
PLEASE!
SNORT
SHHHHH!
HE-HE-HE-HE-HE!
ALMOST DONE...
ALL RIGHT! LET'S GET OUTTA HERE!
HE-HE-HE!
MAID!
Please clean this room

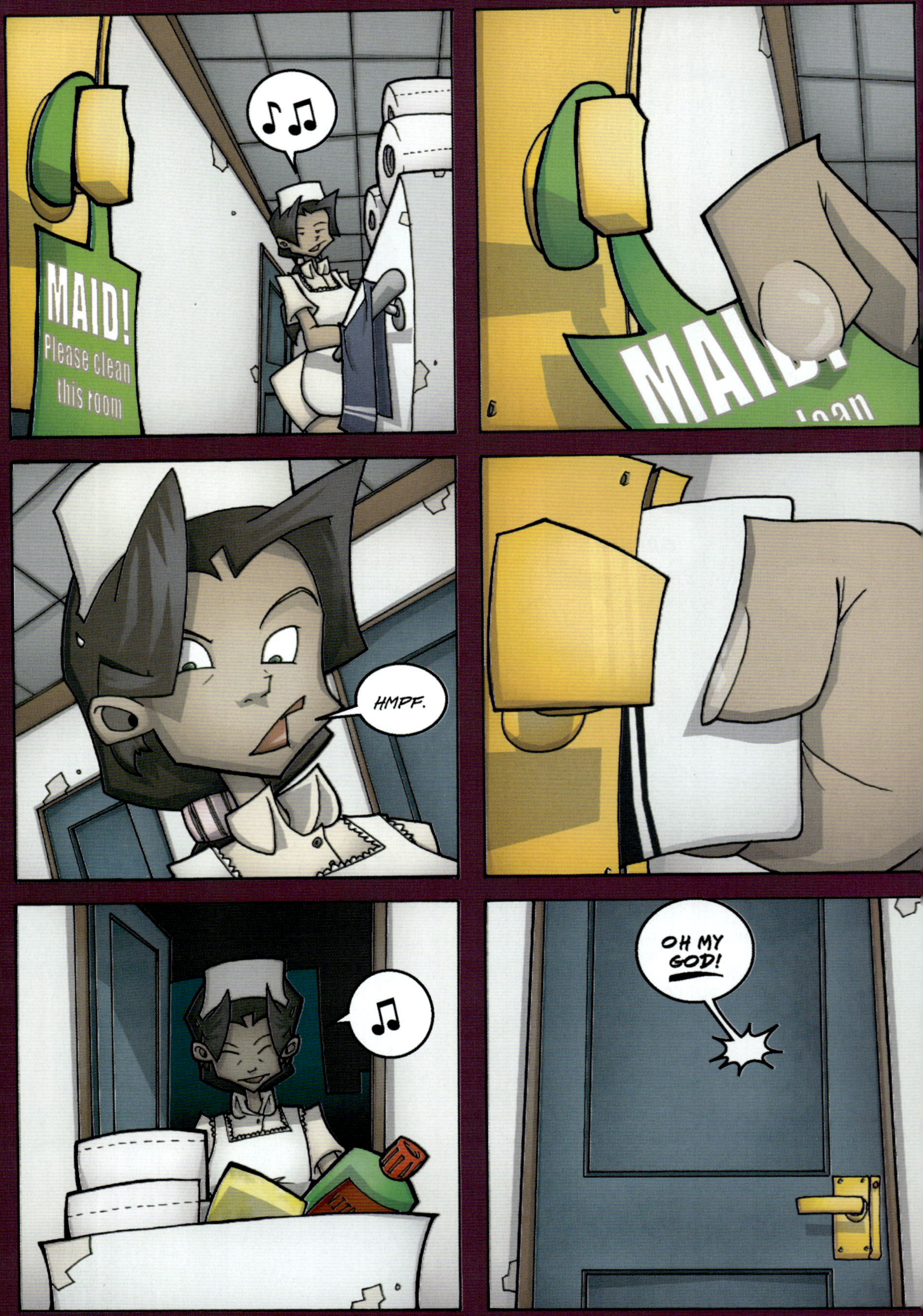
MAID!
Please clean this room
♪♫
MAID!
HMPF.
♫
OH MY GOD!

UH...

THIS ISN'T WHAT IT LOOKS LIKE.

NO?

WELL...

MAYBE IT IS.

I'M CALLING THE POLICE.

WAIT!
PLEASE!
IT'S MY SON!
HE WAS KILLED --
AND THE MAN RESPONSIBLE IS AT THE RESTAURANT RIGHT ACROSS THE STREET!
YOUR SON WAS MURDERED?
NOT EXACTLY, BUT PLEASE...
JUST GIVE ME A CHANCE TO EXPLAIN.

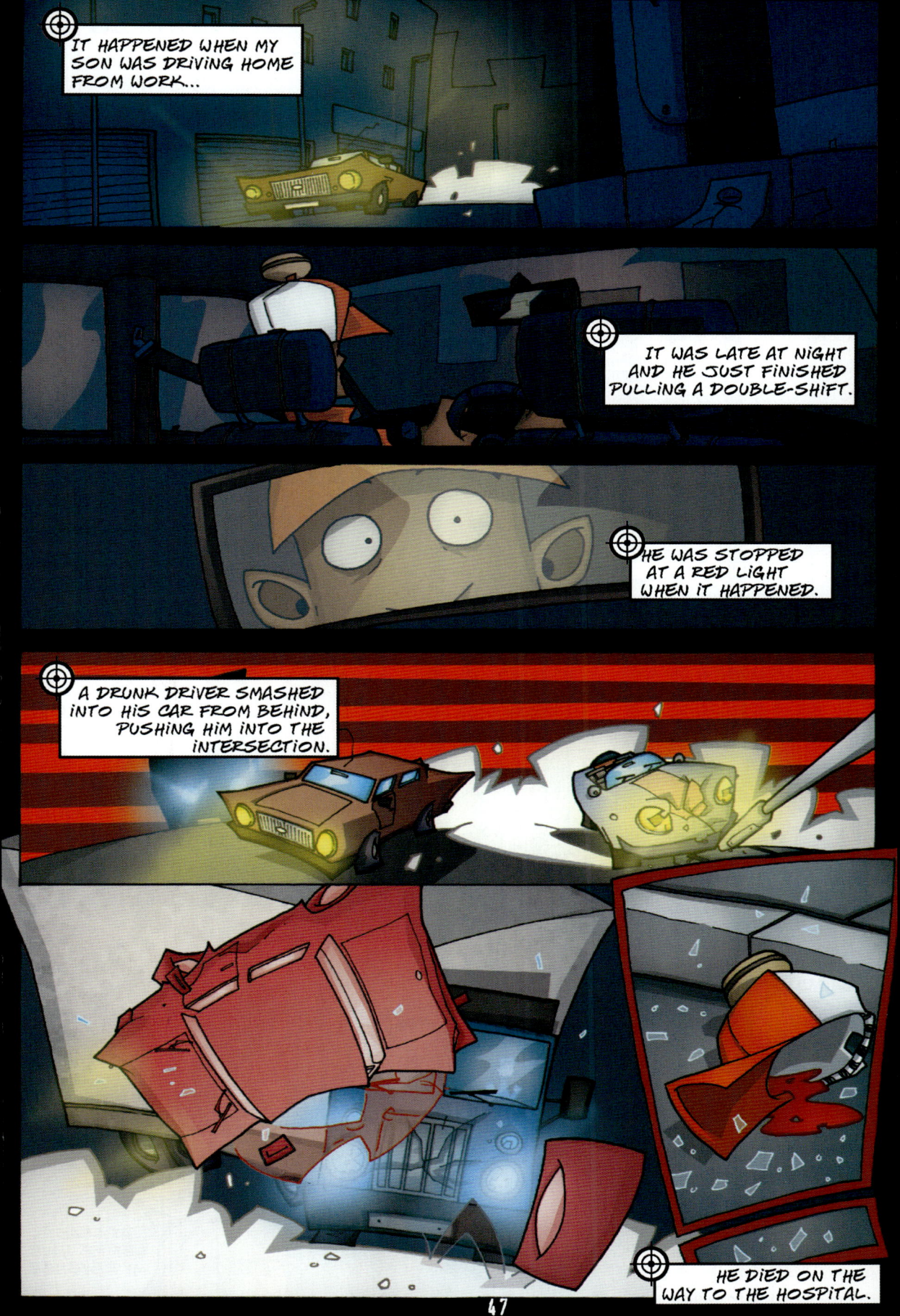

IT HAPPENED WHEN MY SON WAS DRIVING HOME FROM WORK...

IT WAS LATE AT NIGHT AND HE JUST FINISHED PULLING A DOUBLE-SHIFT.

HE WAS STOPPED AT A RED LIGHT WHEN IT HAPPENED.

A DRUNK DRIVER SMASHED INTO HIS CAR FROM BEHIND, PUSHING HIM INTO THE INTERSECTION.

HE DIED ON THE WAY TO THE HOSPITAL.

THE DRIVER WHO STRUCK HIM WAS FOUND ALIVE...

PASSED OUT AT THE WHEEL.

IT WAS HIS SECOND DRUNK DRIVING OFFENSE.

HE BEAT THE FIRST SET OF CHARGES BECAUSE HE COULD AFFORD TO HIRE A VERY HIGH DOLLAR – AND VERY INFLUENTIAL – ATTORNEY.

THAT SAME ATTORNEY IS NOW ENJOYING A FANCY DINNER WITH HIS SON...

WHILE MINE IS DEAD.

PLEASE, I BEG OF YOU...

MY SON IS LOST TO ME FOREVER...

AT LEAST LET ME HAVE MY REVENGE.

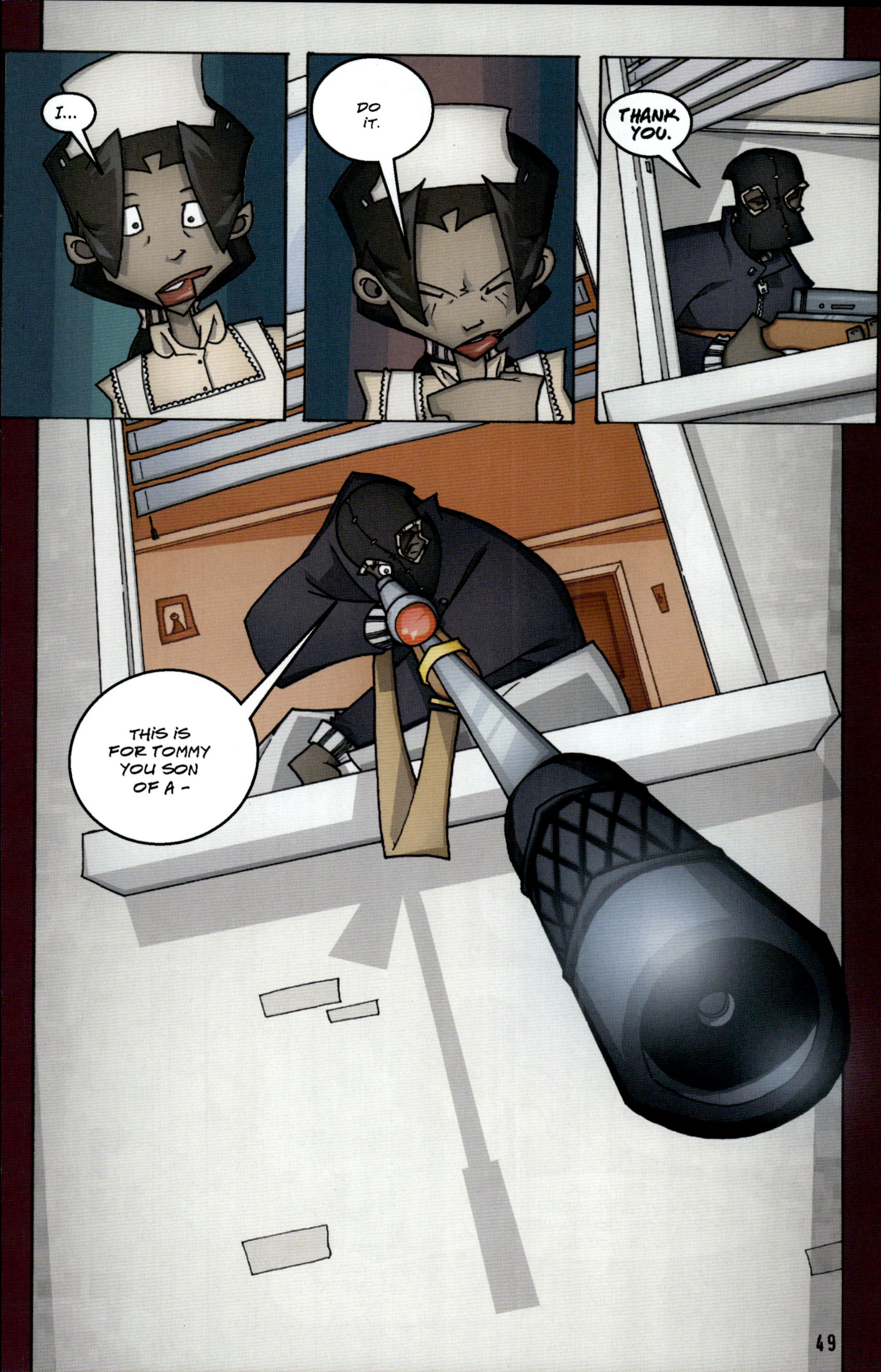
I...
DO IT.
THANK YOU.
THIS IS FOR TOMMY YOU SON OF A -

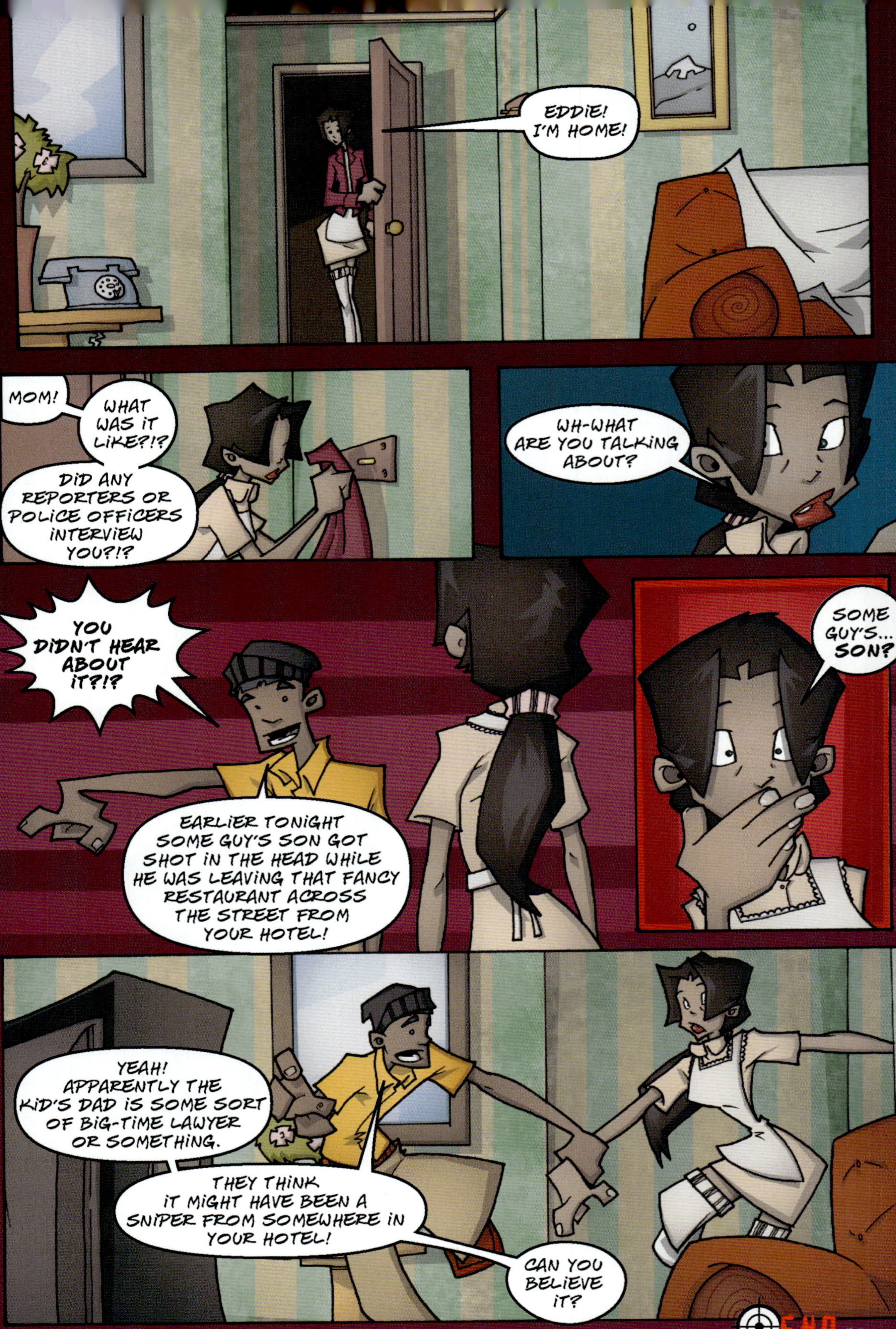
EDDIE! I'M HOME!
MOM!
WHAT WAS IT LIKE?!?
DID ANY REPORTERS OR POLICE OFFICERS INTERVIEW YOU?!?
WH-WHAT ARE YOU TALKING ABOUT?
YOU DIDN'T HEAR ABOUT IT?!?
EARLIER TONIGHT SOME GUY'S SON GOT SHOT IN THE HEAD WHILE HE WAS LEAVING THAT FANCY RESTAURANT ACROSS THE STREET FROM YOUR HOTEL!
SOME GUY'S... SON?
YEAH! APPARENTLY THE KID'S DAD IS SOME SORT OF BIG-TIME LAWYER OR SOMETHING.
THEY THINK IT MIGHT HAVE BEEN A SNIPER FROM SOMEWHERE IN YOUR HOTEL!
CAN YOU BELIEVE IT?
END

NOT FOR YOU
WRITTEN BY AARON WEISBROD
ILLUSTRATED BY KRISTEN "MEREKATY" PERRY
COLORED BY JAIME JONES
LETTERING BY JAMES REDDINGTON
A KING?
REALLY?
WOULD I GET TO WEAR A CROWN AND EVERYTHING?
WAIT!
WHY ARE YOU LEAVING?
COME BACK!
MOM!

AND WHY HAVEN'T YOU COME HOME YET, YOUNG MAN

I BOUGHT YOU THAT WATCH FOR A REASON, PHILLIP.

BUT MOM... I WAS TALKING TO ARKELINA!

OH? AND WHAT DID SHE HAVE TO SAY TODAY?

THAT ME AND HER ARE DESTINY-ED FOR GREAT THINGS TOGETHER!

SHE SAID THAT HARDLY ANYONE CAN SEE HER KIND OF PEOPLE AND THAT WHEN I GROW UP ME AND HER WILL BE EVEN CLOSER FRIENDS THAN WE ARE NOW!

HMMM... IT SOUNDS LIKE SHE THINKS YOU ARE A VERY SPECIAL PERSON.

THAT'S A VERY NICE FLOWER, PHILLIP. DID YOU PICK THAT FOR ME?

giggle

NO! ARKELINA GAVE IT TO ME!

SHE SAID IT'S FROM HER KINGDOM AND THAT WE DON'T HAVE ANY FLOWERS LIKE IT HERE.

52

53

YOU KNOW, THINGS ARE GETTING PRETTY SERIOUS BETWEEN HER AND I.
I DON'T WANT TO DO ANYTHING TO SCREW IT UP AT THIS POINT, YOU KNOW?
ARKELINA?
ARE YOU OK?
YOU SEEM UPSET...
IS IT SOMETHING I --
WHOA!
ARKELINA, WAIT!
WHAT'S WRONG?

HIC
PHILLIP... I CAN'T BELIEVE WE'RE DOING THIS!
WHAT IF MY PARENTS FIND OUT I'M NOT REALLY SPENDING THE NIGHT AT RACHEL'S HOUSE?
HIC
THEY WON'T.
BESIDES, STACY, RACHEL USES YOU FOR HER COVER STORY TO SPEND THE NIGHT WITH HER BOYFRIEND ALL THE TIME!
YEAH, BUT-
SHHHHH...
JUST KISS ME.

YAWN
OH... HEY, ARKELINA.
OH! ARKELINA!
UH... LISTEN...
I CAN EXPLAIN THIS.
WAIT!
DON'T LEAVE!
C'MON! PLEASE!
JUST GIVE ME A CHANCE TO-
EXPLAIN.

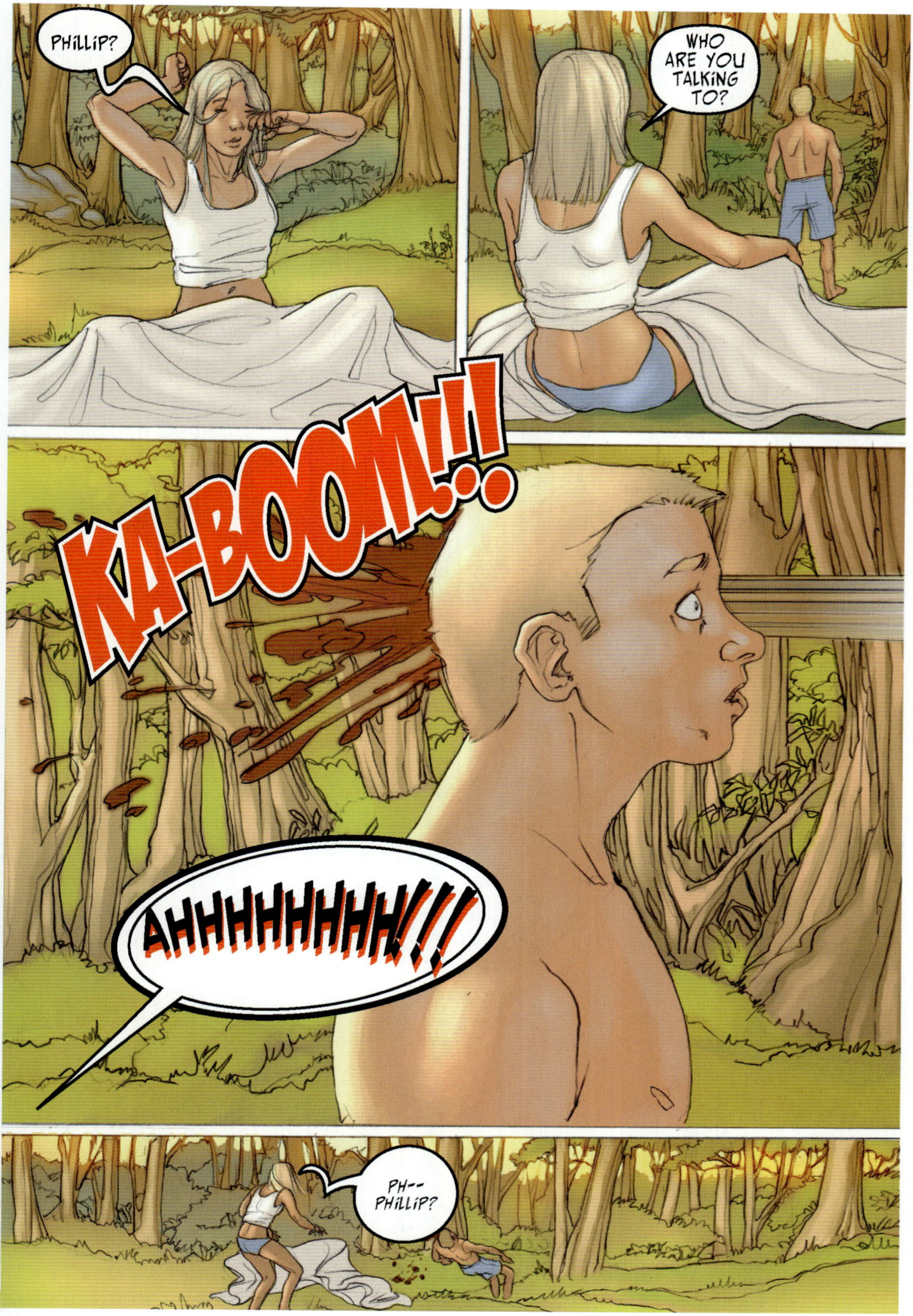
PHILLIP?
WHO ARE YOU TALKING TO?
KA-BOOM!!!
AHHHHHHHH!!!
PH-- PHILLIP?

(Special thanks to Scott Allie)

58

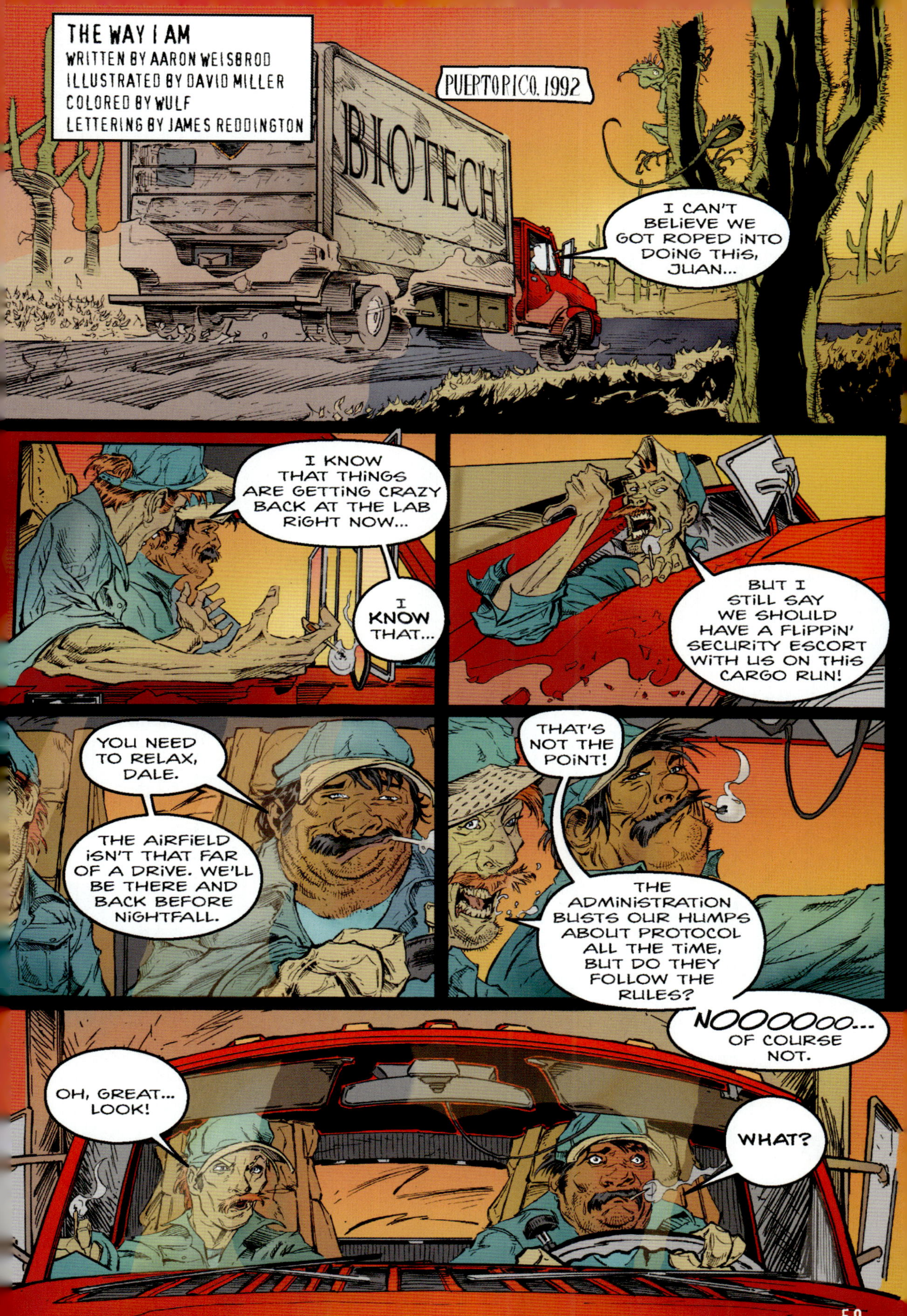
THE WAY I AM
WRITTEN BY AARON WEISBROD
ILLUSTRATED BY DAVID MILLER
COLORED BY WULF
LETTERING BY JAMES REDDINGTON
PUERTO RICO, 1992
BIOTECH
I CAN'T BELIEVE WE GOT ROPED INTO DOING THIS, JUAN...
I KNOW THAT THINGS ARE GETTING CRAZY BACK AT THE LAB RIGHT NOW...
I KNOW THAT...
BUT I STILL SAY WE SHOULD HAVE A FLIPPIN' SECURITY ESCORT WITH US ON THIS CARGO RUN!
YOU NEED TO RELAX, DALE.
THE AIRFIELD ISN'T THAT FAR OF A DRIVE. WE'LL BE THERE AND BACK BEFORE NIGHTFALL.
THAT'S NOT THE POINT!
THE ADMINISTRATION BUSTS OUR HUMPS ABOUT PROTOCOL ALL THE TIME, BUT DO THEY FOLLOW THE RULES?
NOOOOOOO... OF COURSE NOT.
OH, GREAT... LOOK!
WHAT?

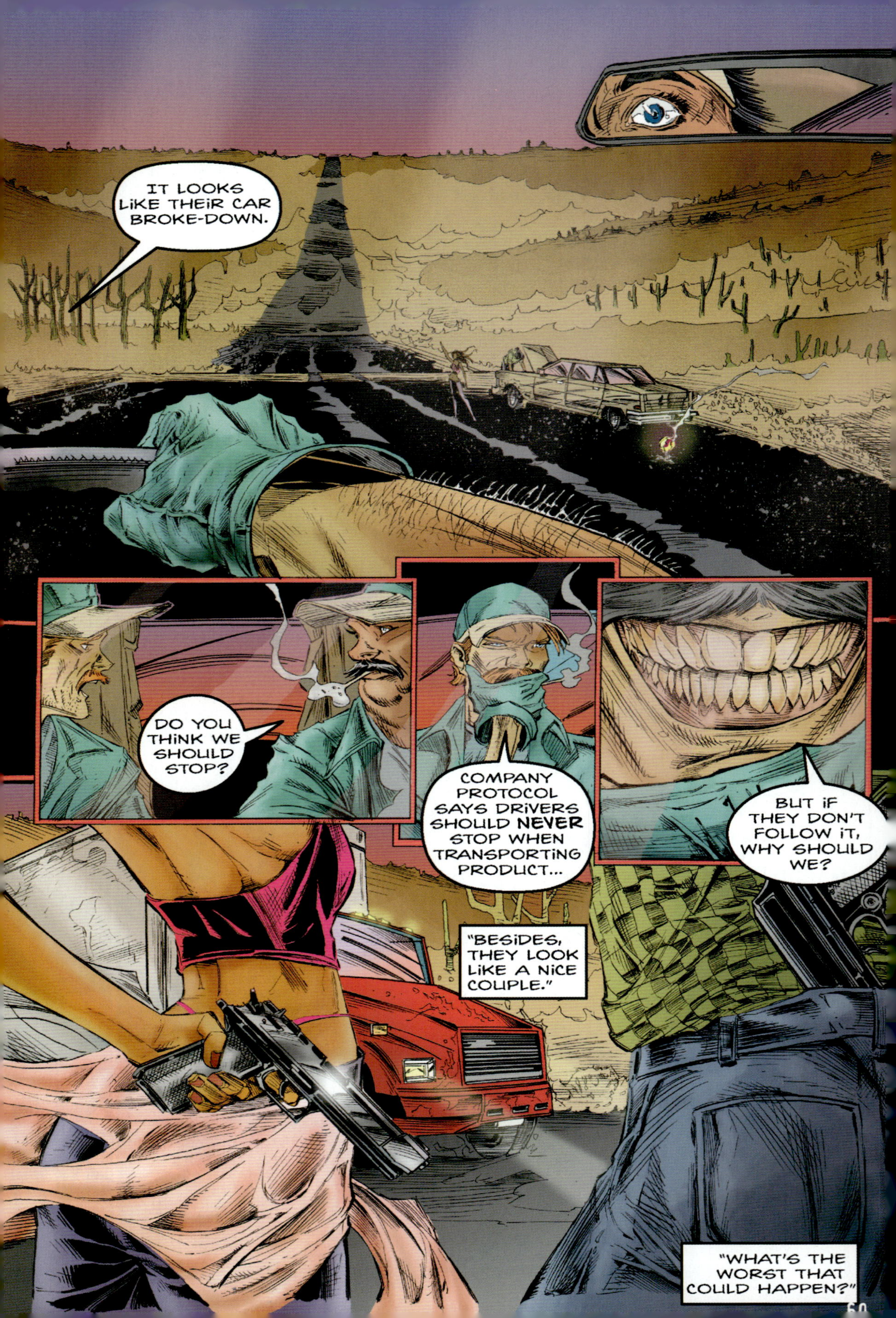
IT LOOKS LIKE THEIR CAR BROKE-DOWN.
DO YOU THINK WE SHOULD STOP?
COMPANY PROTOCOL SAYS DRIVERS SHOULD **NEVER** STOP WHEN TRANSPORTING PRODUCT...
BUT IF THEY DON'T FOLLOW IT, WHY SHOULD WE?
"BESIDES, THEY LOOK LIKE A NICE COUPLE."
"WHAT'S THE WORST THAT COULD HAPPEN?"

I SWEAR, ROSIE, WHY WE EVER SHOT PEOPLE **BEFORE** MAKING THEM DIG **THEIR OWN** GRAVES IS BEYOND ME...

MMMM-HMMM...

WHAT'S THE MATTER, BABY? IS THAT LOCK TOO TOUGH FOR YOUR DELICATE HANDS?

DO YOU NEED YOUR BIG STRONG TONY-BEAR TO HELP YOU, SENORITA?

CLICK

NO.

FINALLY!
NOW LET'S SEE WHAT WE HAVE IN HERE!
IF WE'RE LUCKY IT WILL BE A NICE EXPERIMENTAL VIRUS THAT WE CAN SELL FOR A FEW THOUSAND...
dollars.
Heh.
YOU KNOW, TONY, I DON'T THINK IT'S A VIRUS.
YOU'RE PROBABLY RIGHT, BUT THERE'S ONLY ONE WAY TO FIND OUT!
NO! WAIT!
BLAM!
CHING

BULLSEYE.
YOU LIKE THAT, SENORITA?
IDIOT!!!
WHAT WERE YOU THINKING?
THE BULLET COULD HAVE RICOCHETED BACK AND HIT YOU!
OR WORSE, IT COULD HAVE DAMAGED THE CARGO!
YOU'RE RIGHT, I'M -
HEY!
AIR HOLES... AND THAT SMELL...
THERE'S SOMETHING ALIVE IN HERE.

oh...

my...

DEFINITELY NOT A VIRUS.

YOU HAVE GOT TO BE KIDDING ME!
WE'VE WAITED SO LONG FOR AN OPPORTUNITY LIKE THIS, ONLY TO GET...
I DON'T KNOW...
A PACK OF VAMPIRE-LIZARD-DOGS?!?
LET'S JUST KILL THE LITTLE FREAKS AND GET OUT OF HERE.
DON'T EVEN THINK ABOUT IT.
WHAT'S YOUR PROBLEM, ROSIE?
THEY'RE JUST SOME STUPID LAB EXPIREMENTS! THEY'VE PROBABLY NEVER EVEN BEEN OUTSIDE A CAGE BEFORE!
EXACTLY...

WELL... THERE THEY GO.
ARE YOU HAPPY NOW, ROSIE?
YES.
YOU KNOW, YOU NEVER CEASE TO AMAZE ME.
OH? WHY'S THAT?
WE SURELY COULD HAVE MADE SOME MONEY OFF THOSE CREATURES...
SOMEHOW.
YET INSTEAD YOU CHOSE TO LET THEM GO.
WHY?
BECAUSE I HAVE A SOFT-SPOT FOR WILD ANIMALS, TONY.
IT'S THE WAY I AM.
Less than one month later a Puerto Rican goat farmer reported an attack on his livestock by a small blood-sucking animal that soon became known as "EL CHUPACABRA."
There are now regular Chupacabra sightings in Puerto Rico as well as Argentina, Bolivia, Columbia, Peru, Brazil, Mexico, the Dominican Republic, and the southern United States.
END

SLEEP NOW IN THE FIRE

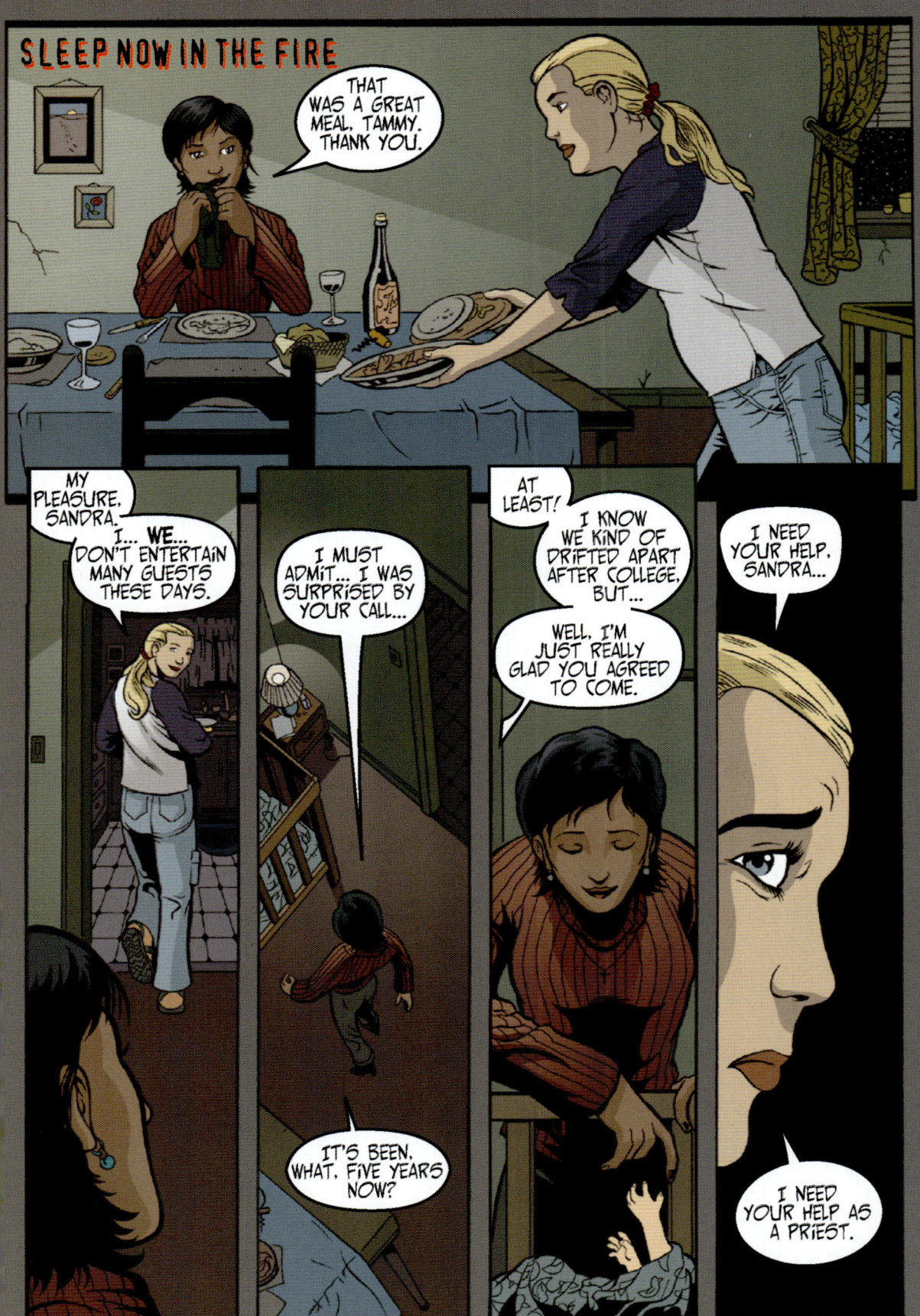

THAT WAS A GREAT MEAL, TAMMY. THANK YOU.

MY PLEASURE, SANDRA. I... WE... DON'T ENTERTAIN MANY GUESTS THESE DAYS.

I MUST ADMIT... I WAS SURPRISED BY YOUR CALL...

AT LEAST! I KNOW WE KIND OF DRIFTED APART AFTER COLLEGE, BUT... WELL, I'M JUST REALLY GLAD YOU AGREED TO COME.

IT'S BEEN, WHAT, FIVE YEARS NOW?

I NEED YOUR HELP, SANDRA...

I NEED YOUR HELP AS A PRIEST.

WRITTEN BY AARON WEISBROD   PENCILED BY JEFF WELBORN   INKED BY CHRIS J. DREIER
COLORED BY DON MACKINNON   LETTERING BY JAMES REDDINGTON

67

I FIGURED AS MUCH.
I'M NOT A PRIEST THOUGH, TAMMY. I'M A *REVEREND.*
THIS IS ABOUT SAMUEL, ISN'T IT?
YEAH.
IT'S ABOUT SAMUEL AND HIS FATHER.
I KNOW YOU'RE NOT MARRIED, BUT IS HE AT LEAST HELPING SUPPORT THE TWO OF YOU?
I COULDN'T SAY THIS BEFOREHAND OR SOMETHING AWFUL WOULD HAVE HAPPENED TO YOU, TAMMY, BUT NOW THAT YOU'RE HERE...
I NEED TO TALK TO YOU ABOUT SAMUEL'S FATHER.
HE'S THE DEVIL.

WHAT?
I KNOW WHAT YOU'RE THINKING, SANDRA, BUT I'M NOT CRAZY.
RESTROOMS
I MET HIM A YEAR AGO WHEN I WAS WORKING DOWNTOWN AT THE OAKMONT INN.
IT WAS ABOUT AN HOUR BEFORE CLOSING TIME WHEN HE WALKED INTO THE BAR.
THERE WAS SOMETHING ABOUT HIM THAT INSTANTLY **INTOXICATED** ME, SANDRA.
IT WAS LIKE LOVE AT FIRST SIGHT... ONLY STRONGER.

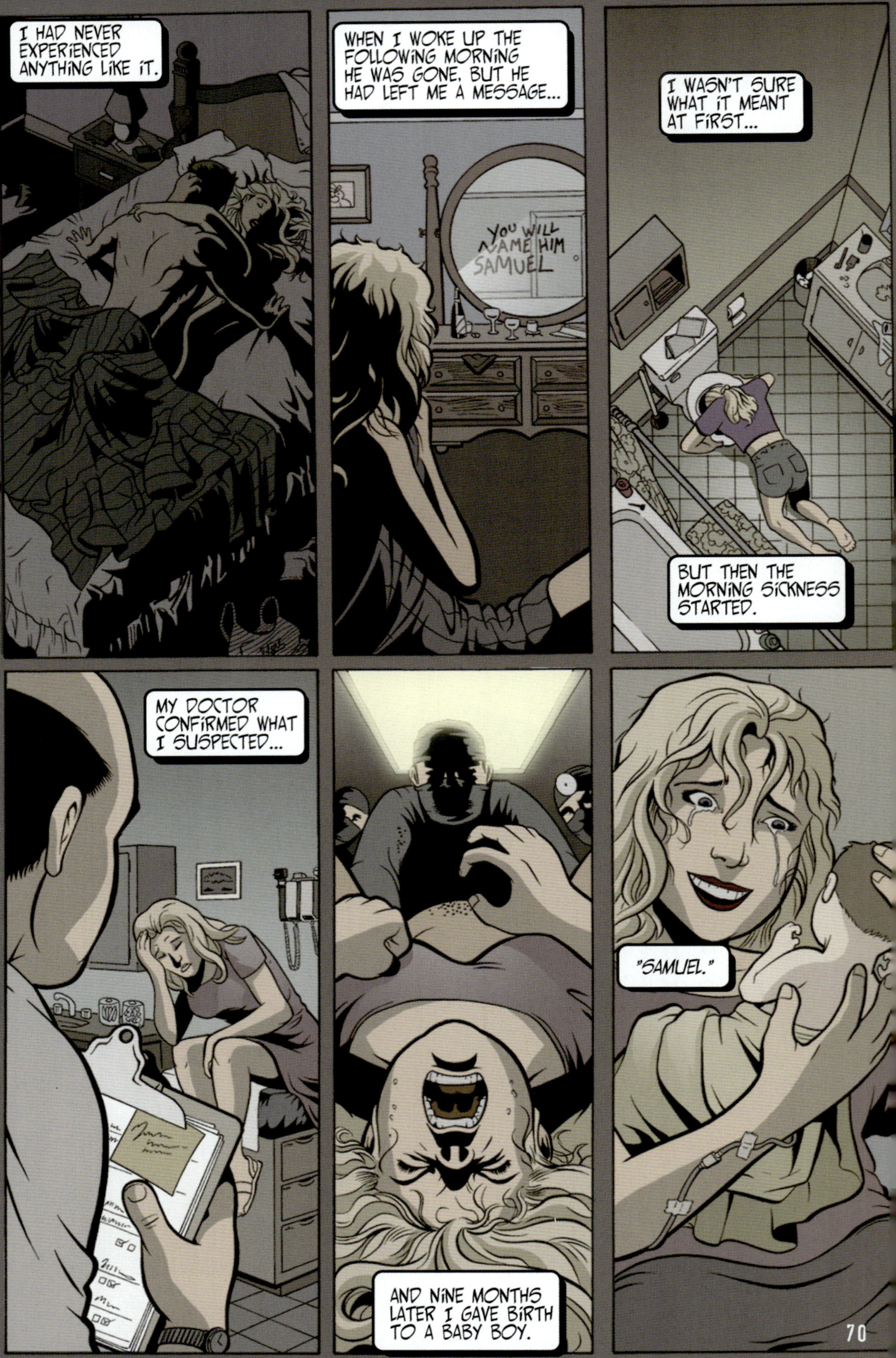
I HAD NEVER EXPERIENCED ANYTHING LIKE IT.
WHEN I WOKE UP THE FOLLOWING MORNING HE WAS GONE, BUT HE HAD LEFT ME A MESSAGE...
YOU WILL NAME HIM SAMUEL
I WASN'T SURE WHAT IT MEANT AT FIRST...
BUT THEN THE MORNING SICKNESS STARTED.
MY DOCTOR CONFIRMED WHAT I SUSPECTED...
AND NINE MONTHS LATER I GAVE BIRTH TO A BABY BOY.
"SAMUEL."

AFTER I GOT BACK FROM THE HOSPITAL I COULDN'T BRING MYSELF TO LEAVE THE HOUSE...
NOT EVEN TO GET SAMUEL BAPTIZED.
SOMETHING WASN'T RIGHT.
I FINALLY MUSTERED-UP THE WILLPOWER TO CALL MONSIGNOR GATES, AND HE AGREED TO COME OVER THAT EVENING.
WHEN HE NEVER ARRIVED I FEARED THE WORSE...
ONLY TO HAVE IT CONFIRMED BY THE ELEVEN O'CLOCK NEWS.
NEWS
DO NOT CROSS POLIC
POLICE LINE - DO NOT CR
LOCAL PASTOR STRUCK BY TRUCK LEAVING CHURCH
I WAS HORRIFIED, BUT IT WAS ALL STARTING TO MAKE SENSE.
I HADN'T BEEN OUTSIDE SINCE COMING HOME...

IT WAS SAMUEL...
SOMEHOW HE - OR HIS FATHER - WAS CONTROLLING ME...
KEEPING ME SHUT-OUT FROM THE OUTSIDE WORLD.
I'M A PRISONER IN MY OWN HOME, SANDRA!
IT'S JUST ME AND THIS... THIS... THING!
THE DEVIL HAS TAKEN OVER MY LIFE!
THERE'S A NATURAL EXPLANATION FOR THE WAY YOU'RE FEELING, TAMMY.
IT'S CALLED POSTPARTUM DEPRESSION. A LOT OF WOMEN EXPERIENCE IT AFTER-
HAVEN'T YOU BEEN LISTENING TO ME?!?
THE DEVIL HIMSELF CAME INTO THE BAR, SEDUCED ME, AND IMPREGNATED ME!
WHEN I TRIED TO GET HELP FROM MY MONSIGNOR HE DIED!
IT'S NOT ALL COINCIDENCE, SANDRA!
YOU'RE A RELIGIOUS PERSON TOO! YOU KNOW THE DEVIL IS REAL!
TAMMY?
YOU'RE DEPRESSED. YOU NEED HELP.
I CAME TO YOU FOR HELP!
please... help me...

TAMMY... DEAR...
YOU DON'T NEED A PRIEST...
YOU NEED A PSYCHOLOGIST.
you don't believe me...
no one will ever believe me...
I BELIEVE HOW YOU FEEL, TAMMY, I DO...
BUT BLAMING YOUR CHILD AND HIS DEADBEAT FATHER... SAYING THAT THIS IS ALL PART OF A CONSPIRACY BY THE DEVIL...
THAT'S NOT FAIR TO YOU OR SAMUEL...
SAMUEL NEEDS YOU, TAMMY.
SAMUEL NEEDS A MOTHER.
YOU'RE RIGHT.
SAMUEL NEEDS A MOTHER.
THAT'S WHAT THIS IS ALL ABOUT.

TAMMY, WAIT...
WHAT ARE YOU DOING?
SAMUEL NEEDS A MOTHER, SANDRA...
TAMMY - STOP!
BUT IT'S NOT GOING TO BE ME.
I'M SORRY.
NO!
OH, TAMMY...
WHY?
WHY?
END

MOVIN' ON
WRITTEN BY AARON WEISBROD
FULLY ILLUSTRATED AND LETTERED BY RAY DILLON

C'MON IN, FRIEND! YOU'RE GONNA FREEZE TO DEATH OUT THERE!

75

THANK YOU!
THINK NUTHIN' OF IT, FRIEND.
YOUR CAR GIVIN' YOU PROBLEMS?
I'M AFRAID SO.
TO MAKE MATTERS WORSE, MY CELL PHONE WON'T EVEN GET A SIGNAL OUT HERE.
THEN YOU'RE EXTRA LUCKY I HAPPENED TO DRIVE BY!
I DON'T KNOW IF YOU HEARD ABOUT IT OR NOT, BUT ***THE SATANIC SLASHER*** IS SUSPECTED TO BE IN THIS VERY AREA!
YES ...
I DO BELIEVE I HAPPENED TO HEAR SOMETHING ABOUT THAT ON THE RADIO ...

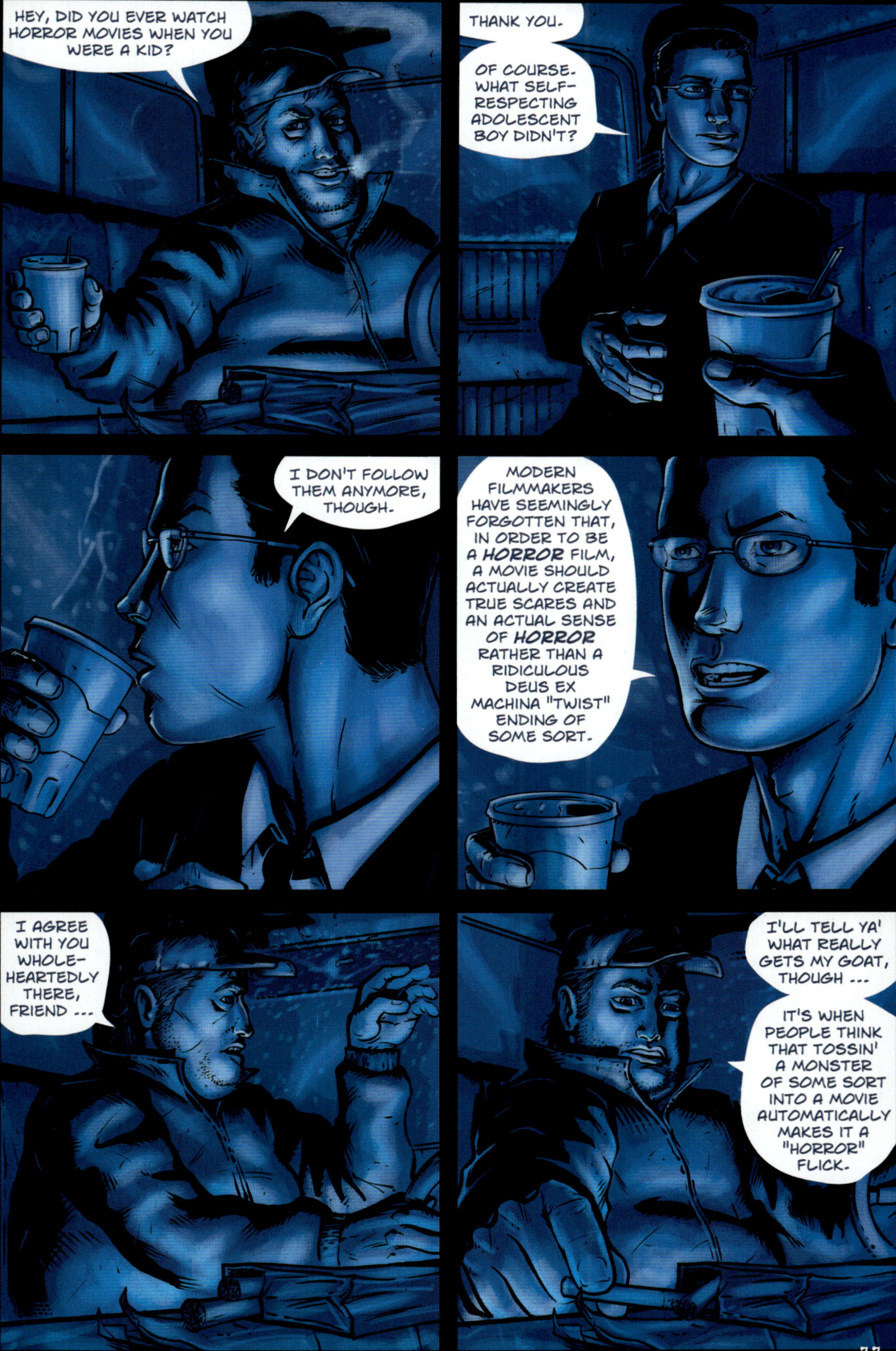
HEY, DID YOU EVER WATCH HORROR MOVIES WHEN YOU WERE A KID?
THANK YOU.
OF COURSE. WHAT SELF-RESPECTING ADOLESCENT BOY DIDN'T?
I DON'T FOLLOW THEM ANYMORE, THOUGH.
MODERN FILMMAKERS HAVE SEEMINGLY FORGOTTEN THAT, IN ORDER TO BE A **HORROR** FILM, A MOVIE SHOULD ACTUALLY CREATE TRUE SCARES AND AN ACTUAL SENSE OF **HORROR** RATHER THAN A RIDICULOUS DEUS EX MACHINA "TWIST" ENDING OF SOME SORT.
I AGREE WITH YOU WHOLE-HEARTEDLY THERE, FRIEND ...
I'LL TELL YA' WHAT REALLY GETS MY GOAT, THOUGH ...
IT'S WHEN PEOPLE THINK THAT TOSSIN' A MONSTER OF SOME SORT INTO A MOVIE AUTOMATICALLY MAKES IT A "HORROR" FLICK.

I MEAN, AT WHAT POINT DID IT BECOME OKAY FOR WRITERS TO BE SO LAZY THAT TOSSIN' A ZOMBIE OR A WEREWOLF INTO A STORY MADE IT "HORROR" RATHER THAN JUST PLAIN OL' LAZY FICTION OR SOME SORT OF WISH- FULFILLMENT POWER- FANTASY CRAP?
1956.
THAT'S WHEN "GODZILLA: KING OF THE MONSTERS" WAS RELEASED HERE IN THE UNITED STATES.
AMERICAN SOCIETY AT LARGE FAILED TO REALIZE THAT THE BEAST WAS MEANT TO BE A SYMBOL FOR THE ATROCITY OF THE ATOMIC BOMB, HENCE KICKING THE MONSTER-MOVIE CRAZE INTO AN IRREVOCABLE HIGH GEAR.
HEH.
YOU REALLY SEEM TO KNOW YOUR MONSTERS, FRIEND.
AND THAT'S GOOD.
TRUTH BE TOLD, I CONSIDER MYSELF AN EXPERT ON THEM TOO.
OH?
YEAH.
IN FACT, I KNOW THAT THERE ***JUST-SO-HAPPENS*** TO BE A MONSTER IN THIS HERE TRUCK RIGHT NOW.

SO ... HOW YOU FEELIN' OVER THERE, FRIEND?
A LITTLE ...
WOOZY?
YEAH, WELL, THAT'S TO BE EXPECTED.
THERE ARE ENOUGH TRANQUILIZERS IN THAT COFFEE TO KNOCK-OUT AN ELEPHANT.
YOU WERE DONE FOR WITH YOUR FIRST SIP.
WHY?
HAW-HAW-HAW!

"WELL, IT WEREN'T SO I COULD GO ON AND TAKE ADVANTAGE OF YA', IF THAT'S WHAT YOU'RE THINKIN'!

NAH... I GOT NEWS FOR YA', FRIEND.

YOU'RE ABOUT TO BECOME THE TWENTY-THIRD VICTIM OF NONE OTHER THAN...

THE SATANIC SLASHER!!!

NO...

I'M NOT.
ROOFIES IN THE COFFEE.
AHHH!!!
AHHH!!!
IT'S A GOOD TRICK.
ONE I OFTENTIMES USE MYSELF.
A WORD TO THE WISE?
NEVER TAKE A DRINK FROM ANYONE.
AFTER ALL, THERE ARE A LOT OF DANGEROUS PEOPLE OUT THERE IN THE WORLD.
MORE THAN YOU EVEN CARE TO IMAGINE.

WHAT THE--?!?
IMPOSSIBLE!
IT COULDN'T BE ...
COULD IT?
THE CARVINGS ... THEY'RE ALMOST IDENTICAL!
A COPYCAT!
MY WORK, MY VISION, MY DREAM ...
IT SUDDENLY SEEMS SO ... PASSE.
DAMN THE INTERNET!
CAN NOTHING BE KEPT A SECRET ANYMORE?
HEY, YOU NEED A LIFT OR SOMETHING?
I'VE HAD A GOOD RUN ...
BUT PERHAPS IT'S TIME TO MOVE ON ...
-8-
END

WELCOME TO MY NIGHTMARE

WRITTEN BY AARON WEISBROD
ILLUSTRATED BY JOSH ROSS
COLORS BY -3-
LOGO BY JAMES REDDINGTON

83

-FIN-

THE MINUTE OF DECAY
WRITTEN BY AARON WEISBROD
FULLY ILLUSTRATED BY MARK MATLOCK
LETTERING BY JAMES REDDINGTON

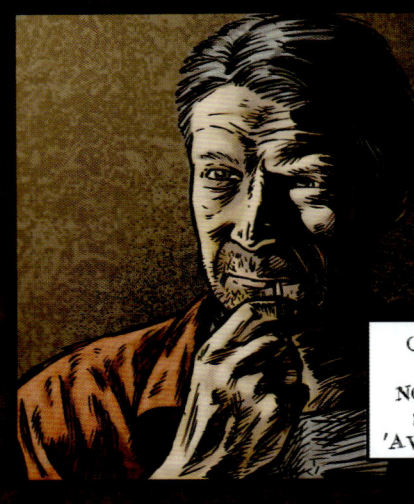

OF COURSE I KNOW NOW THAT I SHOULDN'T 'AVE DONE IT.

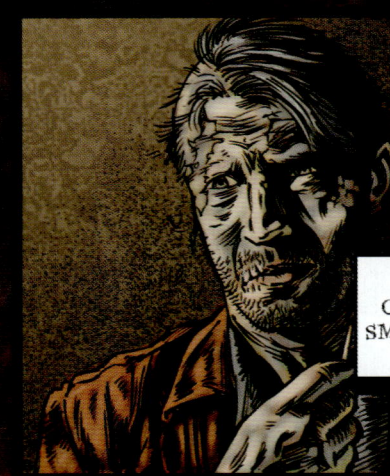

I MEAN, REALLY, WHO WAS I TO THINK THAT I COULD TRICK 'IM?

STUPID... BLOODY STUPID.

I'M SURE A LOT OF BLOKES MUCH SMARTER THAN ME 'AVE TRIED...

PEOPLE WITH MORE BRAINS.

MMM... BRAINS.

END

DISASTERPIECE
WRITTEN BY AARON WEISBROD
ILLUSTRATED BY JOSH ROSS
COLORED BY DON MACKINNON
LETTERING BY JAMES REDDINGTON
HMF.
I SEE YOU HAVE NOT LOST YOUR FLAIR FOR THE DRAMATIC, JAMES.
THIS IS A WORTHWHILE EVENT, IS IT NOT?
AFTER ALL THESE YEARS OF COMBAT AND POSITIONING, OUR FEUD WILL FINALLY END TONIGHT.
AT LONG LAST...
I WILL RULE THE WORLD.
NO!
YOU'VE STOOD IN MY WAY LONG ENOUGH!
OUR FEUD WILL END TONIGHT, BUT WITH ME AS THE VICTOR!
I ASSURE YOU, BRIAN, BY THE END OF THIS NIGHT THE WORLD WILL BE MINE, NOT YOURS
ARROGANT FOOL!
YOU HAVE NO IDEA OF THE LENGTHS I AM WILLING TO GO TO ASSURE VICTORY!
NOR DO YOU OF ME.

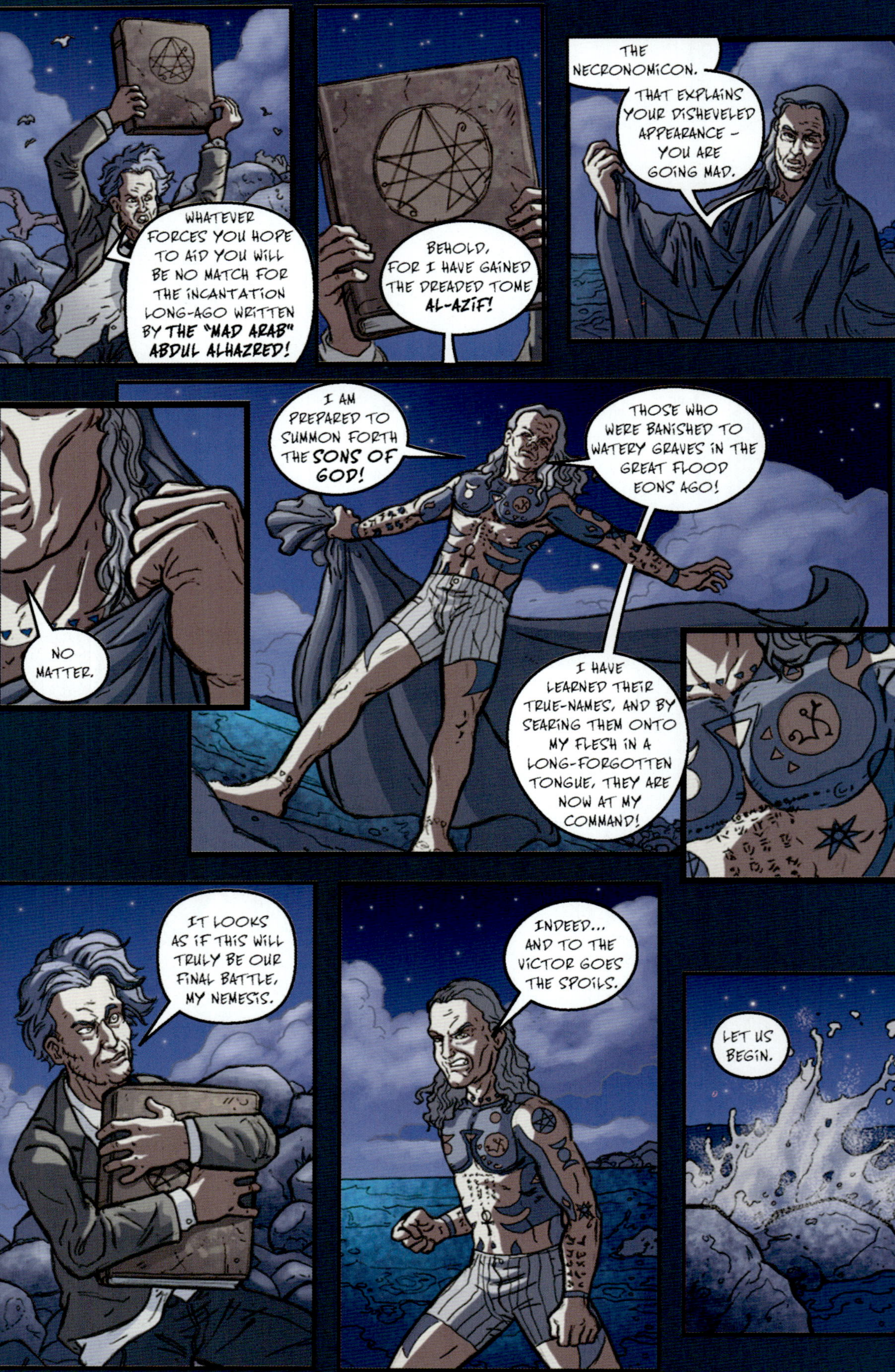
WHATEVER FORCES YOU HOPE TO AID YOU WILL BE NO MATCH FOR THE INCANTATION LONG-AGO WRITTEN BY THE "MAD ARAB" ABDUL ALHAZRED!
BEHOLD, FOR I HAVE GAINED THE DREADED TOME AL-AZIF!
THE NECRONOMICON.
THAT EXPLAINS YOUR DISHEVELED APPEARANCE - YOU ARE GOING MAD.
NO MATTER.
I AM PREPARED TO SUMMON FORTH THE SONS OF GOD!
THOSE WHO WERE BANISHED TO WATERY GRAVES IN THE GREAT FLOOD EONS AGO!
I HAVE LEARNED THEIR TRUE-NAMES, AND BY SEARING THEM ONTO MY FLESH IN A LONG-FORGOTTEN TONGUE, THEY ARE NOW AT MY COMMAND!
IT LOOKS AS IF THIS WILL TRULY BE OUR FINAL BATTLE, MY NEMESIS.
INDEED... AND TO THE VICTOR GOES THE SPOILS.
LET US BEGIN.

IA! IA! ZI AZAG! IA! IA!! ZI AZKAK! IA! IA! CTHULHU ZI KUR! IA!
O THOU THAT LIETH DEAD BUT EVER DREAMETH!
MAY ETERNAL SLUMBER HINDER YOU NO LONGER!
I SUMMON YOU FORTH! HERE MY PLEA! DESTROY MY MOST HATED ENEMY AND GRANT ME ULTIMATE POWER!!!
SONS OF GOD!
TRUE INHERITORS OF THE EARTH!
THEY WHO WERE BEFORE THE GREAT FLOOD!
I SUMMON THEE FORTH!
RISE FROM YOUR GRAVES IN THE DEPTHS OF THE ABYSS!
HEAR ME AND RISE!

And so began the battle that would bring about the end of the world.

The long-forgotten titan-spawn brought forth by the lust of angels for mortal women...

Versus an alien monstrosity who sought to reclaim the earth for his own extra-dimensional kin.

Animals around the world began to cry out in the night.

Small children everywhere began tossing restlessly in their sleep.
Mankind's final hour was at hand.
But was it really these two power-hungry humans who were unknowingly orchestrating Armageddon...
Or had their long-enduring feud finally outgrown them...
Taking-on a life of its own?

Some events, once started, quickly grow beyond our control.

These things happen.

But who's REALLY to blame?

Why do we let those who clamor for power set into motion the means to destroy us?

Is it apathy?

Fear?

A sense of helplessness?

No excuse is good enough...

Yet we still let them do it.

Don't get me wrong... to want to rule the world is one thing...

But to damn us all in the process?
That is another matter entirely.
end

COVERS

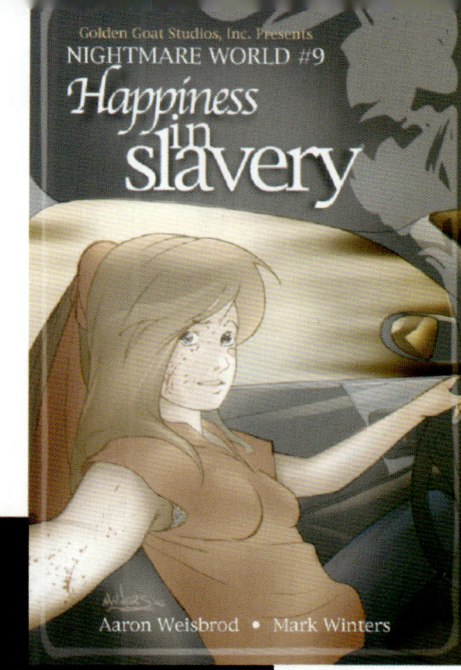

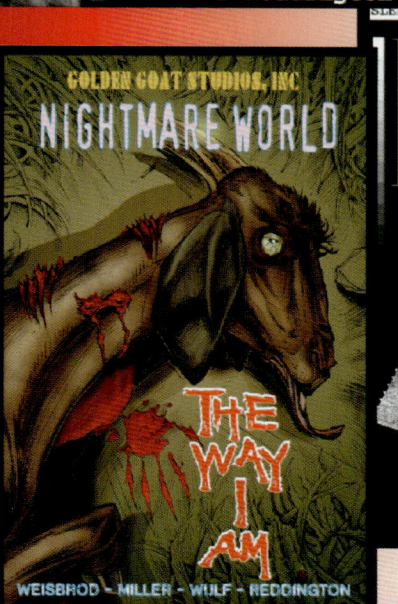

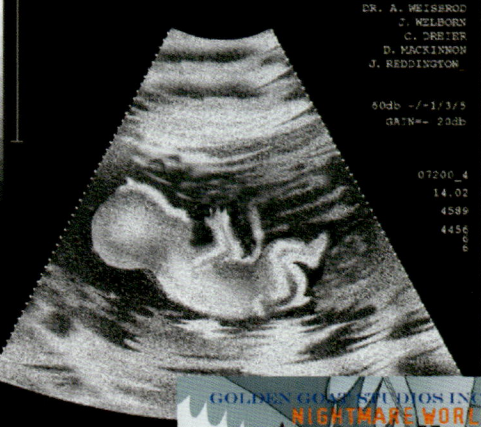

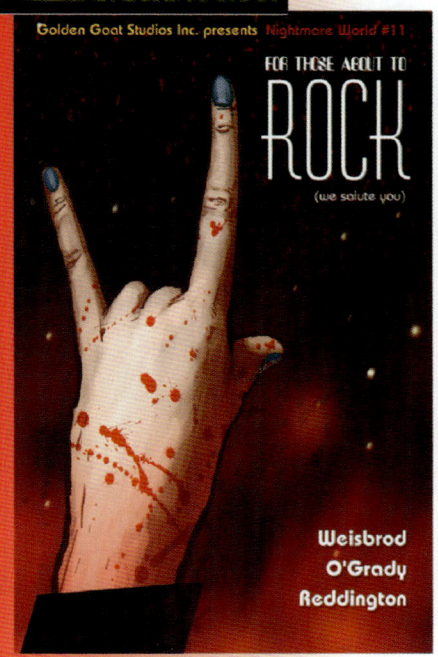

93

COVERS

ABOUT THE AUTHOR...

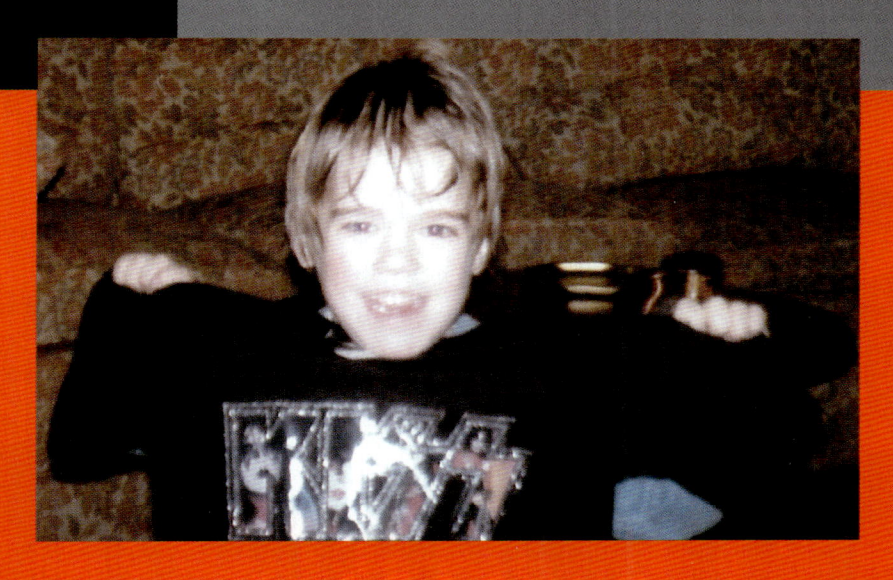

Brought into this world on January 30, 1975, Aaron Weisbrod was born nine days late and has been trying to make up for the lost time ever since. As of this writing he is an accomplished high school teacher on the verge of completing his second Master's Degree in Education, a freelance comicbook and music journalist, a 1st Degree Tae Kwon Do instructor, an established community theater director, a loving husband, a friend to children and small animals everywhere, a loud and proud member of **Golden Goat Studios** and **Grafika Press**, and the writer/creator of **Nightmare World**.

Aaron Weisbrod loves life but hates ninjas. Cthulhu is his homeboy. His three main vices in life are books, female heavy-metal singers, and comics signed by Alan Moore. He **still** fears the toilet monster. He watches very little TV. His wife calls him a "sexy geek." She's half right.

GOLDEN GOAT STUDIOS, INC. PRESENTS
www.NIGHTMAREWORLD.com

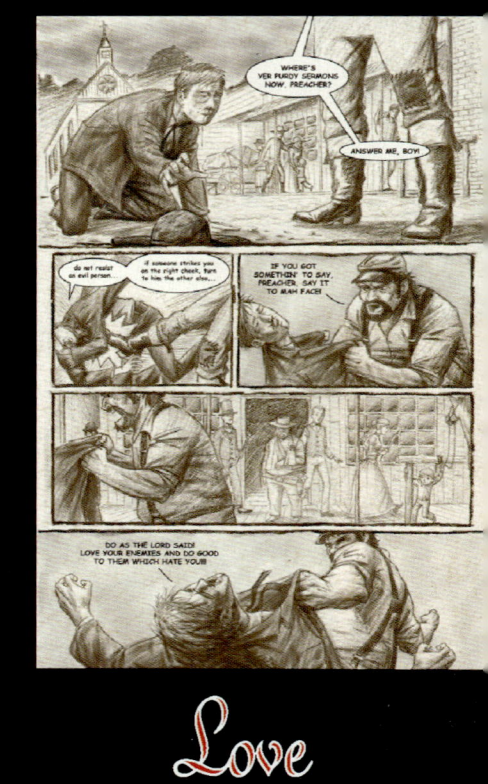

Life

Love

THURSDAYS

Horror

DEATH